The Spy Goddess novels
by Michael P. Spradlin

Spy Goddess, Book One:
Live and Let Shop

Spy Goddess, Book Two:
To Hawaii, with Love

The Spy Goddess manga

Spy Goddess, Volume One:
The Chase for the Chalice

SPY GODDESS

Volume Two
The Quest for the Lance

Created by
Michael P. Spradlin

Script by
Johanna Stokes

Illustrated by
Rainbow Buddy

HAMBURG // LONDON // LOS ANGELES // TOKYO

HARPER
An Imprint of HarperCollinsPublishers

Spy Goddess Vol. 2: The Quest for the Lance
Created by Michael P. Spradlin
Script by Johanna Stokes
Illustrated by Rainbow Buddy

Lettering - Lucas Rivera and Fawn Lau
Cover Illustration - Rainbow Buddy
Cover Design - Jose Macasocol, Jr.

Editor - Luis Reyes & Jenna Winterberg
Digital Imaging Manager - Chris Buford
Pre-Production Supervisor - Erika Terriquez
Production Manager - Elisabeth Brizzi
Managing Editor - Vy Nguyen
Creative Director - Anne Marie Horne
Editor-in-Chief - Rob Tokar
Publisher - Mike Kiley
President and C.O.O. - John Parker
C.E.O. and Chief Creative Officer - Stuart Levy

A  **TOKYOPOP** Manga

TOKYOPOP and 🐟 are trademarks or registered trademarks of TOKYOPOP Inc.

TOKYOPOP Inc.
5900 Wilshire Blvd. Suite 2000
Los Angeles, CA 90036

E-mail: info@TOKYOPOP.com
Come visit us online at www.TOKYOPOP.com

Library of Congress Catalog Card Number: 2009922792

ISBN: 978-0-06-136300-9

09 10 11 12 13   LP/WOR   10 9 8 7 6 5 4 3 2 1
❖
First Edition

CONTENTS

Chapter One............................6

Chapter Two...........................32

Chapter Three........................57

Chapter Four..........................82

Chapter Five.........................107

Chapter Six..........................132

Chapter One

OKAY, RACHEL, YOU BARELY ESCAPED GOING TO JUVIE BY BECOMING A SPY AT BLACKTHORN ACADEMY.

AND SIMON BLANKENSHIP, A NUT JOB WHO THINKS HE'S THE REINCARNATION OF THE BULL GOD MITHRAS, HAS IT IN FOR YOU BECAUSE HE THINKS YOU'RE THE REINCARNATED GODDESS ETHEREA.

AND NOW YOU HAVE TO KICK HIS BUTT IN AN ANCIENT MITHRIAN TEMPLE...

...WITH SOME KILLER MANOLO BLAHNIKS.

OKAY, HOLD IT. LIGHTS, PLEASE.

MR. KIM, I CAN TOTALLY FIGHT MY WAY PAST THEM.

THEN I'D SAY SHE FAILED.

NOT EXACTLY THE OUTFIT OF A COVERT OPERATIVE.

THE POINT OF A COVERT OP EXERCISE ISN'T TO SEE IF YOU CAN FIGHT, RACHEL.

IT'S TO SEE IF YOU CAN AVOID FIGHTING.

THERE'S NO LAW AGAINST LOOKING HOT WHILE FIGHTING EVIL.

BESIDES, SIMON COULD STRIKE AT ANY TIME. I HAVE TO BE READY NO MATTER WHAT I'M WEARING.

WELL. UM. I'M NOT EXACTLY SURE.

WELL, SINCE IT'S OUR STRONGEST LEAD, I VOTE WE HEAD TO BRAZIL TONIGHT AND FIGURE THE REST OUT ON THE WAY.

GOOD IDEA. AND AFTER WE LOCATE THE ARTIFACT, MAYBE WE CAN FIND THAT PESKY NEEDLE IN THAT SILLY OL' HAYSTACK THAT EVERYONE'S ALWAYS LOOKING FOR.

ACTUALLY, ONCE IN BRAZIL WE'LL BE ABLE TO ACCESS RECORDS THAT AREN'T AVAILABLE ONLINE AND THEY MIGHT POINT US IN THE RIGHT DIRECTION.

15

PILAR'S RIGHT.

AND BY MOVING QUICKLY, WE HAVE A VERY GOOD CHANCE OF BEATING SIMON TO SOME OF THESE ARTIFACTS.

I WISH WE COULD BEAT HIM TO ALL OF THEM...

I WISH WE COULD JUST BEAT HIM.

YES, WELL, THE POINT IS, HE CAN'T COMPLETE THE RITUAL WITHOUT *ALL* THE ARTIFACTS SO HAVING EVEN A FEW WILL HELP EVEN THE PLAYING FIELD.

MIND IF I SIT DOWN?

WHY DON'T YOU HAVE YOUR GIRLFRIEND READ MY MIND AND FIND OUT.

RACHEL, PLEASE.

I'M ABOUT TO GO TO SLEEP.

NO YOU AREN'T.

AND HOW DO YOU KNOW THAT?

YOU ONCE SAID FASHION MAGAZINES ARE LIKE CAFFEINE FOR YOU.

IF YOU FLIP THROUGH ONE AT BEDTIME, YOU'LL BE UP ALL NIGHT.

I CAN'T HELP IT IF NEW SEASON TRENDS GET MY HEART RACING.

IT'S YOUR KEEN POWERS OF OBSERVATION THAT WILL ONE DAY MAKE YOU A GREAT DETECTIVE.

LISTEN, I KNOW WE HAVEN'T EXACTLY BEEN BEST FRIENDS SINCE YOU ARRIVED.

29

NOTHING! JUST... JUST STRATEGY AND STUFF.

RIGHT, ALEX?

RIGHT. JUST TALKING STRATEGY.

OKAY.

I SHOULD GET BACK UP THERE. SO... IS EVERYTHING OKAY?

THANKS.

YEAH. EVERYTHING'S GREAT.

Chapter Two

BOA VINDA A BRAZIL

PILAR, WHY DON'T YOU GO BUY SOME MAPS AND TOURIST BOOKS

SO WE KNOW WHICH LIBRARY OR MUSEUM TO HIT FIRST.

AND BRENT, YOU GO HAIL A CAB WHILE I EXCHANGE OUR MONEY.

SEE? THEY DON'T EVEN NEED ME.

LET'S SIT FOR A MOMENT AND TALK.

UH-OH.

JUST SIT DOWN.

33

RACHEL, I KNOW YOU'VE BEEN THROUGH A LOT. PROBABLY MORE THAN THE REST OF US PUT TOGETHER.

AND I'M NOT GOING TO LIE TO YOU. IT'S NOT GOING TO GET ANY EASIER. SO IF YOU DON'T THINK YOU'RE UP FOR THIS...

I GET IT.

BECAUSE OF MY OUTBURST BACK AT BLACKTHORN YOU THINK I'M LOSING IT. BUT I'M NOT DESERTING YOU GUYS.

AND I'M SORRY FOR ACTING THAT WAY.

IT'S JUST HARD. I DIDN'T ASK FOR ANY OF THIS.

AS YOU KNOW...

AND I KNEW I COULDN'T JUST SIT AROUND HOPING HE DIDN'T COMPLETE HIS QUEST...

...OR THINKING SOMEONE ELSE WOULD STEP IN AND DEFEAT HIM.

...I WAS WITH SIMON WHEN HE FOUND THE BOOK THAT STARTED ALL OF THIS AND I WATCHED HIS DESCENT INTO MADNESS AS HE BECAME OBSESSED WITH RESURRECTING MITHRAS.

NO.

I'M TELLING YOU THIS TO REMIND YOU THAT YOUR FRIENDS DO HAVE A CHOICE IN THE MATTER.

AND YET... THEY CHOOSE TO BE HERE. WITH YOU.

OH.

SO MAYBE THEY'RE THE ONES YOU NEED TO BE APOLOGIZING TO?

NUTS.

OH. WELL...

I BELIEVE HE DID.

...HE SHOULD HAVE SAID SOMETHING.

TRY THAT. IT'S AN ELECTRONIC TRANSLATOR.

BRENT, WAIT!

UM... UH...

?

SET IT TO ENGLISH/ PORTUGUESE AND THEN YOU CAN TYPE OR SPEAK A PHRASE AND IT WILL TRANSLATE IT FOR YOU

AH!

SO... HOW EXACTLY DOES THIS WORK?

AND IT WILL TRANSLATE WHAT OTHERS ARE SAYING TO YOU, AS WELL.

44

45

LET'S GET GOING.

ALL RIGHT.

HEY.

REALLY GREAT WORK, PILAR.

I DON'T KNOW WHAT WE'D DO WITHOUT YOU.

ANY DECENT PERSON WOULD DO THE SAME.

I'M JUST HONORING A COMMITMENT.

48

BUT WE HATE EACH OTHER.

YES, THANK YOU.

I AM AWARE OF THAT.

I MEAN, WE DON'T HATE-HATE EACH OTHER.

I JUST MEAN WE DON'T EXACTLY GET ALONG.

I MEAN, WE DON'T THINK ABOUT EACH OTHER IN THAT WAY... DO WE?

NO! NO, OF COURSE NOT.

. . . . .

IT'S JUST...

...SHE SAW US TOGETHER IN THE BACK OF THE PLANE AND WE DIDN'T HAVE A GOOD EXCUSE FOR WHY WE WERE SO CLOSE...

BECAUSE YOU WOULDN'T LET ME TELL HER THE TRUTH!

I KNOW, I KNOW. THIS IS ALL MY FAULT. I GET IT.

SO YOU'D RATHER YOUR BEST FRIEND THINK YOU'RE TRYING TO STEAL HER BOYFRIEND?

JUST FOR RIGHT NOW. JUST TILL I FIGURE A FEW THINGS OUT. OKAY?

FINE. COME ON, THEY'RE WAITING FOR US.

IS IT TIME TO TAKE A BREAK, YET?

I SUPPOSE WE COULD TAKE FIVE MINUTES TO USE THE LAVATORY.

AND BRENT AND I WILL GO ROUND UP SOME SNACKS.

DON'T YOU WANT TO TAKE A BREAK?

NO, THANK YOU.

PILAR, I KNOW YOU'RE MAD AT ME AND I JUST WANT TO SAY I'M SORRY...

...FOR FREAKING OUT ON YOU GUYS BACK AT BLACKTHORN.

I'M NOT UPSET ABOUT THAT.

THEN WHAT IS IT? YOU'VE BEEN ACTING WEIRD SINCE THE PLANE.

ALEX AND I REALLY WERE JUST TALKING.

YES! I SWEAR.

IS THAT RIGHT?

SO YOU'RE NOT KEEPING ANYTHING FROM ME THEN?

NO.

I GUESS MAYBE YOU'VE FORGOTTEN I CAN TELL WHEN SOMEONE IS LYING TO ME.

PILAR...

NO, RACHEL. YOU DON'T WANT TO COME CLEAN? FINE.

BUT DON'T SIT HERE AND LIE TO ME.

!

I'VE GOT WORK TO DO. GO HIT THOSE BRAZILIAN MARKETS OR SOMETHING.

PILAR, LISTEN...

THAT'S WHAT YOU'RE BEST AT.

Chapter Three

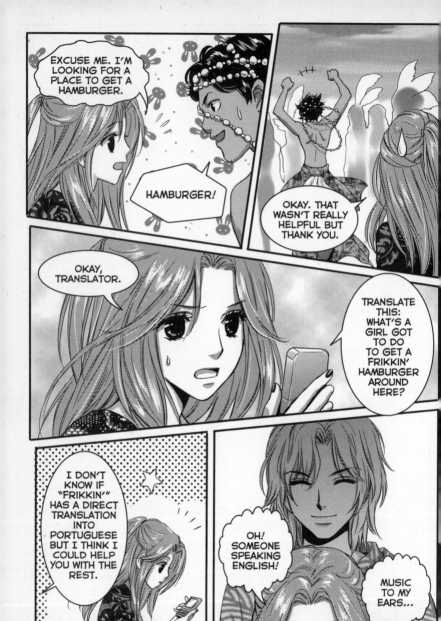

HI. I'M RENARD.

AND YOU ARE?

IN LOVE.

UM, I MEAN, I'M RACHEL.

NO...

I'M GUESSING YOU'RE NOT FROM AROUND HERE.

...I'M FROM AMERICA.

I'LL CALL THE HOTEL, SEE IF SHE'S IN THE ROOM.

I'M TRYING HER CELL.

RING RING

DO YOU NEED TO GET THAT?

RING

Pilar

NOPE.

Click

64

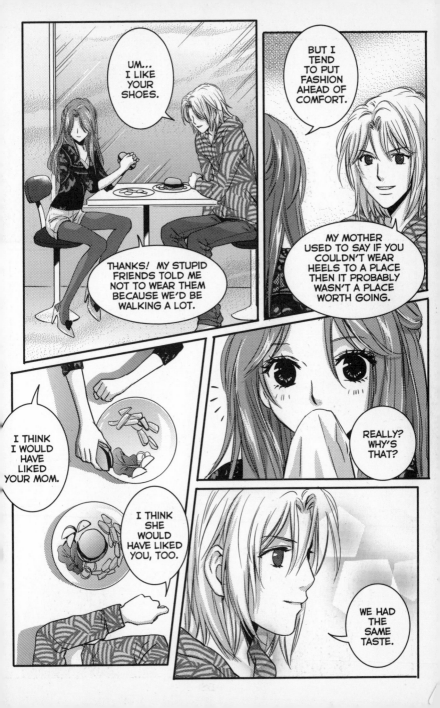

HATE TO INTERRUPT YOUR DATE.

ALEX! WHAT ARE YOU DOING HERE?

LOOKING FOR YOU.

WHAT'S THE MATTER?

WHAT'S THE MATTER?

YOUR FRIENDS HAVE BEEN WORKING FOR THE BETTER PART OF TEN HOURS WHILE YOU'RE OUT PICKING UP FOOD...

...AMONG OTHER THINGS.

I DIDN'T PICK HIM UP, ALEX.

I WAS LOST AND HUNGRY AND HE ESCORTED ME TO THIS RESTAURANT.

SAVE IT, RACHEL. I DON'T CARE WHAT YOU TWO ARE DOING...

WE'RE NOT DOING ANYTHING!

WE WERE JUST WORRIED ABOUT YOU, BUT I CAN SEE YOU'RE TAKING CARE OF YOURSELF.

JUST LIKE ALWAYS.

ARE YOU... IN LOVE WITH HIM?

WHAT?!? NO!!!

IT'S JUST...

...WELL, WE GO TO SCHOOL TOGETHER AND WE HAVE THE SAME FRIENDS AND WE'RE ALL PART OF THIS GROUP AND THE GROUP DEPENDS ON ME.

RACHEL, YOU HAVE TO DO WHAT YOUR HEART TELLS YOU TO DO.

BUT I REALLY WISH YOU'D STAY.

...CRY OF THE BULL.

84

WHEN I FIGURED OUT THE ARTIFACT HAD TO BE ON THIS MOUNTAIN, I JUST RAN OFF. I DIDN'T EVEN THINK TO GIVE HIM MY NUMBER.

OH NO!

YEAH. IT'S LIKE WEARING YOUR FAVORITE SANDALS TO THE BEACH AND THEN LOSING THEM IN THE SAND.

GUYS! ENOUGH SHOE TALK.

WE NEED TO STAY FOCUSED. WE'RE LOOKING FOR SOME SORT OF ENTRANCE INTO THE MOUNTAIN BUT WE DON'T HAVE ANY IDEA WHERE IT IS.

SURE WE DO.

IT'S RIGHT OVER THAT RIDGE.

IT'S OKAY, GUYS. I'M FINE.

WELL, DON'T EVERYONE RUSH TO HELP ME UP OR ANYTHING.

SORRY, RACH. IT'S JUST...

WHAT?

OH.

INCREDIBLE.

TRANSLUCENT, CONSTANTLY SHIFTING,

GASEOUS ON A MOLECULAR LEVEL YET SOLID AS STONE.

I CAN SEE THE LANCE.

WE DON'T.

BUT HOW DO WE GET TO IT?

I DO.

RACHEL? CAN YOU HEAR ME?

CAN YOU—

I DON'T THINK YOU CAN HEAR ME, PILAR. BUT IF YOU CAN, DON'T WORRY.

THIS WILL ONLY TAKE A SECOND.

TO PROTECT THIS PLACE I BUILD A WALL...

...OF TIME AND SPACE AND INVISIBLE TO ALL...

...SAVE FOR THOSE WITH EYES TO SEE, AND IMPENETRABLE TO ALL BUT ME.

GUYS? HELLO?

HOW LONG WAS I UNCONSCIOUS?

NOT NEARLY AS LONG AS YOU'RE GOING TO BE.

HELLO, ETHEREA.

WHERE ARE THEY?

WHAT HAVE YOU DONE WITH THEM?

...AND NEW.

DON'T WORRY. THE GANG'S ALL HERE. OLD FRIENDS...

Chapter Five

TO BE FAIR, I NEVER LIED TO YOU.

I JUST NEVER TOLD YOU THAT THE MAN I MET IN AMERICA WAS YOUR MORTAL ENEMY, SIMON BLANKENSHIP.

THAT'S A PRETTY BIG THING TO LEAVE OUT!

WELL, I'D PROMISE TO MAKE IT UP TO YOU LATER, BUT I DON'T THINK YOU'RE GOING TO BE AROUND THAT LONG.

TIME TO HAND OVER THE LANCE, ETHEREA.

DON'T CALL ME THAT!

WAIT! DON'T HURT HER. YOU CAN HAVE THE STUPID THING.

RACHEL...

I'M SORRY, ALEX.

YOU MAY HAVE THE LANCE, BUT THERE ARE OTHER ARTIFACTS YOU NEED AND I'M BETTING THEY'RE ALL PROTECTED LIKE THIS ONE.

AND I'M THE ONLY ONE WHO CAN WALK THROUGH THOSE BARRIERS.

FACE IT BLANKENSHIP...

...YOU NEED US.

ACTUALLY, IF YOU HADN'T SHOWN UP WE WERE GOING TO DIG THROUGH THE MOUNTAIN AND GET TO THE ARTIFACT FROM THE OTHER SIDE.

WOULD IT TAKE LONGER? YES. BUT THE RESULT WOULD BE THE SAME.

YOU SEE, MY DEAR, WHERE THERE'S A WILL, THERE'S A WAY.

AND WHEN EVERY ARTIFACT IS GATHERED...

...THE WORLD WILL KNOW THE NAME MITHRAS!

I WILL BE ALL POWERFUL!

THE UNIVERSE WILL TREMBLE AT MY FEET!

GOD, DOES THAT GUY EVER SHUT UP?

RACHEL, ARE YOU OKAY?

EXCEPT FOR THIS HEADACHE AND THE "I'M ABOUT TO BE KILLED" PART.

I'M SORRY I GOT YOU KIDS INTO THIS.

I'M SORRY WE LET YOU DOWN.

IT'S NOT OVER, YET, YOU GUYS.

IT WAS ABOUT ME...

BUT FIRST, WE MUST TEND TO THE BUSINESS AT HAND...

...AND THE FACT THAT I CAN DO THIS!

GOOD-BYE, BRAZIL.

I FEEL LIKE WE HARDLY GOT TO KNOW YOU AT ALL.

MAYBE NEXT TIME WE COME WE CAN SKIP THE LIBRARY AND MOUNTAIN CLIMBING...

...AND JUST CUT STRAIGHT TO THE MUSIC, FOOD, AND DANCING.

SO WHAT HAPPENS NOW?

NOW WE GO HOME AND START TRYING TO LOCATE THE OTHER ARTIFACTS.

EVEN IF THEY PUT HIM AWAY FOR 20 YEARS, HE'LL REMAIN UNDETERRED FROM HIS GOAL.

YEAH. HE'LL GET OUT EVENTUALLY AND IT'S NOT LIKE HE'S GOING TO BE LESS CRAZY WHEN HE DOES.

WILL THAT REALLY BE NECESSARY, CONSIDERING?

LOOKS LIKE WE'VE GOT EVERYTHING WE NEED, MR. KIM. JUST WANTED TO COMMEND YOU AGAIN.

WELL, THANK YOU BUT ALL THE CREDIT GOES TO THE KIDS. THEY DID AN INCREDIBLE JOB.

THEY SURE DID. I FEEL LIKE I SHOULD TELL YOU THAT THIS KIND OF WORK IS NOT FOR CHILDREN.

BUT CONSIDERING WE'VE BEEN UNABLE TO LOCATE HIM FOR SIX MONTHS, I GUESS I'D JUST END UP SOUNDING FOOLISH.

AND SINCE WE HAVE HIM NOW, I'M HOPING IT WILL NO LONGER BE AN ISSUE. GREAT JOB, KIDS.

WATCH YOUR HEAD.

AND IF I WERE YOU, BLANKENSHIP, I'D ENJOY THE SUN WHILE YOU CAN.

WITH THE CHARGES WE HAVE AGAINST YOU, YOU MAY NEVER SEE IT AGAIN.

RACHEL, I JUST WANTED TO SAY... I KNOW THIS CAN'T BE EASY.

AND NONE OF US WILL EVER REALLY UNDERSTAND WHAT YOU'RE GOING THROUGH.

ARE YOU KIDDING? I'M GREAT. THE NEW LINE OF JIMMY CHOOS JUST CAME OUT!

HEY. HOW YA DOING?

UM, I WAS KIND OF REFERRING TO THE OTHER STUFF.

OH, YEAH. WEIRD, RIGHT?

RACHEL, IT WAS MORE THAN WEIRD. IT WAS INCREDIBLE.

LET'S NOT MAKE A BIG THING OUT OF IT, OKAY?

I'M JUST GLAD IT'S OVER AND WE CAN PUT ALL OF THIS—AND I DO MEAN ALL OF THIS—BEHIND US AND FOCUS ON MORE IMPORTANT THINGS...

...LIKE SUMMER DRESSES AND STRAPPY SANDALS...

...AND FRIENDSHIPS.

The End

SPY GODDESS

Michael P. Spradlin is the captivating author of all the novels and manga volumes of the Spy Goddess series. He lives in Michigan with his family, but his not-so-secret mission is to entertain readers across the globe with his high-action, thrill-packed Spy Goddess adventures. You can visit him online at www.michaelspradlin.com.

Johanna Stokes is a North Carolina native who, after graduating from the University of North Carolina at Chapel Hill, moved to Los Angeles, CA, and has been working in comics and TV ever since. She wrote stories for *Zombie Tales* and *Cthulhu Tales* and co-wrote *Mr. Stuffins* and *Savage Brothers* for BOOM! Studios. Her graphic novel *Station* was optioned by CBS Films for a feature film and her most recent comic book co-creation, *Galveston*, will be released Summer 2009. She worked as a staff writer on the first two seasons of the Sci-Fi Channel hit series *Eureka* and just received a script order for a series she co-created for Showtime.

CLASSIFIED INFORMATION

Name: Yifan Ling
Known Aliases: Ivy,
    Rainbow Buddy
Gender: Female
Date of Birth: Jan. 8, 1983

Location: Beijing, China
Blood type: A
Family members: Parents
Pet: Shiu-Shiu (Shetland
    sheep dog)

Yifan Ling was born in Beijing, China, and started learning to draw at the age of four. In middle school, she fell in love with manga and started trying to draw it. After four years of learning industrial design at a university, Yifan followed her manga dream to the UK and enrolled in the M.A. course of visual communication (illustration) at the Birmingham Institute of Art and Design.

After graduation, Yifan moved to London and her work soon began appearing in UK publications. While in London, Yifan made a connection with TOKYOPOP and one of the results is in your hands now.

Yifan's many manga influences include *Tokyo Babylon, Love Hina, Ranma 1/2, Mars,* and *Fullmetal Alchemist.*

TO HAWAII, WITH LOVE

There is a crazy man after me. Not just your normal crazy man, either. Not some simple ordinary type of crazy, like a celebrity stalker or someone who gets messages from outer space. This is a guy who thinks that he can *rule* the *world*. We're talking Adolf Hitler–type looniness here.

Many years ago this guy accidentally discovered an ancient temple in a Middle Eastern desert that was once dedicated to a Roman god named Mithras. When he discovered the temple, either he unleashed some kind of supernatural force that made him nutso or his obsession with what he found caused him to check himself into the Crazy Hotel.

Oh, and did I also mention that he thinks I'm the living reincarnation of the Goddess Etherea? I told you: wacko. Anyway, whatever he thinks or however he came to think it, the main thing is he wants me dead. Somehow he's got the idea that I'm the only thing standing between him and world domination.

His name is Simon Blankenship. For many years he was a member of an elite, clandestine group of U.S. secret agents called the Blackthorn Squad, along with my headmaster and teacher, Jonathon Kim. Mr. Kim was with Blankenship when he discovered the temple, but whatever happened in there didn't make *him* crazy. I know this because Mr. Kim is probably the most centered and noncrazy person I know.

Mr. Kim is the headmaster at Blackthorn Academy, the boarding school in Pennsylvania that I attend. Well, "attend" is not exactly the right word. Saying you "attend" a school would imply that you had a choice in whether or not to go there, whereas I really didn't. See, I was in a little trouble with the law and this judge said I could either go to the school or go to Juvenile Detention. Since I figured that a young girl from a wealthy Beverly Hills family wouldn't do so well in Juvie, I chose the school. Yep. I fought the law and the law won. I've been here for just about two months now and it's been "interesting," to say the least.

I discovered that the school secretly sits on top of one of the most sophisticated crime labs and secret-agent hangouts in the world. That's because Mr. Kim, the former secret agent, established the school to train students to become members of a worldwide network devoted to stopping Blankenship and his Mithrians. Some of the upperclassmen here at Blackthorn, the ones who belong to the "Top Floor" section, go on missions with agents to help with surveillance or sting operations. That's way cool. Mr. Kim won't let me into Top Floor yet, but I'm wearing him down.

Along with some of the other students here I also helped Mr. Kim recover a very rare, ancient book that Blankenship had tried to steal. Of course, it turned out that Mr. Kim had actually switched the books ahead of time, so Blankenship ended up with a fake. Only, Blankenship doesn't know it's fake. He thinks it's real. Which is a good thing for us.

That was when Blankenship, who now calls himself Mithras, swore that he would seek his revenge on me. Like I said, he thinks that I am the reincarnation of the goddess Etherea, who, according to legend, was sent by the gods to banish Mithras to the underworld.

Did I mention he was crazy?

"No, Rachel, you must cock your hip first, then sweep your arm like this and throw the attacker across your leg, like this," said Mr. Kim. He grabbed the front of my *do bak* and sent me sprawling to the mat. I felt the air whoosh out of my lungs. Again.

From where he was watching, Alex Scott let out a chuckle. Alex is a second-degree black belt in Tae Kwon Do, and while he's pretty strong and brave and stuff, he's really kind of a pain in my backside. He's always laughing at me, because for the most part, I'm a total klutz. I gave him my best stink-eye as I struggled back to my feet.

Brent Christian, who was almost a black belt, stood next to Alex. Brent was different. He was quiet, soft-spoken, and gentle, and he never laughed at me when I exhibited my less-than-graceful nature. Also, it didn't hurt that he has this kind of young Colin Farrell look going, either.

It was 7 A.M. and I was in the school's *do jang*, taking another private Tae Kwon Do lesson from Mr. Kim. Since all the fuss with Blankenship, Mr. Kim had decided that we needed to accelerate my martial arts training. So I met him at 6:30 every morning in the *do jang*, where he drilled me relentlessly on the patterns and taught me self-defense moves. Alex and Brent came along most mornings to help out.

There were two problems with this as far as I was concerned. The first was that I am not a morning person. It was bad enough that everyone at Blackthorn is an early-riser, go-getter type. I mean, they serve breakfast at eight o'clock for crying out loud. I can't possibly form a coherent thought before 10 A.M. The second problem was that since Mr. Kim had started these "extra training sessions," most of the "extra training" involved me landing on my keister. Because Mr. Kim is a Ninth Dan in Tae Kwon Do, an Aikido master, and not only that, he is a personal friend of Jackie Chan. Needless to say, I was a little overmatched. But Mr. Kim felt it was important that I learn as much as I could, as fast as I could.

I stood there for a moment, hands on my knees, trying to get my breath while shooting daggers at Alex. I don't like being laughed at, and he seemed to think my training is all a big joke. He'd told me earlier that I didn't have the "martial arts mentality." I'd replied that I thought it was amazing that he could use three such big words in the same sentence and congratulated him on his improving verbal skills. So now he was a little sore at me. Hence the chuckling while Mr. Kim tossed me around like I was his own personal cat toy.

Speaking of Mr. Kim, he stood waiting for me to straighten up. I thought maybe a question would stall him before he sent me on another short flight across the room.

"Mr. Kim?" I said.

"Yes?"

"You told me that the only way to stop Simon Blankenship would be to find him first, right?"

"You are correct."

"Well, how are we going to do that? I mean, how are we going to find him when he has followers all over the world and a million places to hide and we never know where he is?"

Mr. Kim straightened his *do bak* and then, almost faster than I could see, he launched a spin kick. But this time I was ready, and since he was only going at about half speed, I was able to catch his kicking leg with my crossed arms and, at the same time, sweep his standing leg from under him with my foot and send him to the mat. Takedown, Rachel Buchanan! I couldn't believe I had done it. Soon I'd be starring in the remake of *Fists of Fury*. Hah! I gave Alex a smirk and was very pleased to see the look of total disbelief on his face. Brent smiled and gave me a big thumbs-up. He had a pretty cute smile when he smiled, which wasn't often.

"Excellent, Rachel! First rate!" Mr. Kim bounced back up quickly and beamed a big smile at me. "You showed excellent reflexes. Self-defense is a matter of planning ahead. When someone approaches you, someone who may be a potential foe, you must learn to subconsciously do a 'threat assessment.' If that person is an attacker, what are they likely to try first? From which direction might they launch a strike? Continually ask yourself those questions and eventually it will become second nature." Alex was shaking his head and staring at the floor.

Mr. Kim was still smiling. "How did you anticipate my kick?" he asked.

I paused for a moment and closed my eyes, replaying the sequence in my mind. I saw Mr. Kim straighten his *do bak* and then launch the kick. But wait. While he had straightened his uniform, his weight had shifted to his left leg as he prepared to kick with his right.

"I saw your weight shift right before you kicked. I knew something was coming, and it gave me a chance to prepare," I said.

"Excellent. You see what I mean? You can learn to do this almost without thinking, so you are always ready."

"Okay," I said, "but still, you were only at about half speed. If you'd been going full out, I never would have seen that kick coming," I said.

"Two things, Rachel. First, don't be negative. You did something well. Accept that. Second, you are correct, my skills in

Tae Kwon Do far surpass yours at this point, but not everyone you meet in battle will have my level of skill. Most attackers are clumsy and unbalanced. In time, they will pose little threat to you. With enough study, you may reach Ninth Dan yourself."

Sure, and I also might open for Avril Lavigne. But he did have a point. Not the part about becoming Ninth Dan, but that in the last two months I had trained hard and I was getting better at this. To Alex's shock, I'd progressed all the way to a green belt. I mean, I'm still a klutz for the most part, but I was improving.

Wait a minute. Did he say "meet in battle"? *Battle?* Gulp.

Mr. Kim bowed and told me that the session was over for the day.

"Not so fast, mister," I said. "You still haven't answered my question. How are we going to find Blankenship?"

Mr. Kim smiled. "We will find him by letting him find us," he said. Huh?

"I'm sorry, is that some kind of Zen thing? I don't get it."

Mr. Kim laughed. I crack him up. (Most of the time.)

"There are two things Simon wants in this world. Since we received his e-mail swearing vengeance on you, we know that one of those things is you. Can you guess what the other thing is?"

Mr. Kim is always doing that "answer a question with a question" thing. I hate that.

"Frequent-flyer miles?"

Mr. Kim chuckled again. "No, I'm sure free air travel is the least of Simon's worries. He needs the seven Mithrian treasures for his plan to work. If Simon can get his hands on those artifacts, he believes he will be able to summon the forces of Mithras and unleash them on the world. We have been working on the final translations in the *Book of Seraphim*. If we can decipher some of the riddles, we will know where to look for the relics. Then perhaps we can set a trap for Simon."

Setting traps sounded good. As long as the trap was like totally airtight and I was a long way away from the trap when it was sprung. Several states away from the trap, maybe.

"But if he somehow gets word that we've found a relic, something that's been missing for thousands of years, won't he be suspicious? Won't he try to set a trap for us instead?"

"Of course he will be wary. Simon is very intelligent and determined."

"Not to mention a total freak-a-zoid," I interrupted.

"Yes, that too. But he is also greedy and thirsting for power. That will make him careless. With the right circumstances and the right object, Simon should find himself unable to resist."

Alex and Brent stood there with their heads moving back and forth, watching us talk, like Mr. Kim and I were playing tennis.

"But what if we can't decipher the secrets of the book? Then what? We sit around and wait until somebody finds an artifact that we think he'll be interested in? That could take years," Alex said. Alex wasn't the patient type. In that respect I guess we were a bit alike.

"Remember, Alex, we must be cautious. Simon is a dangerous and deadly man. True, understanding the secrets of the book will not be easy. Scholars in Kuzbekistan have studied the book for years. And while many of the words have been translated, the meaning is often not clear. Our advantage is that it will be just as unclear to Simon and when we have what we need . . ."

Yada yada yada. He said some other stuff about how we must wait until the time is right and not be hasty and all that, but by then I had tuned him out. I'm a teenager, after all.

"I hate waiting," I said. Which was remarkably self-aware on my part, I thought. I'm absolutely no good at waiting. I open my birthday presents early. I'm first in line at the dessert table. I never wait for anything to go on sale.

"Yes, I've learned this about you. But perhaps something will happen sooner than you think." Mr. Kim bowed and dismissed me. I could swear that there was a twinkle in his eye. That meant he was up to something and he was keeping it to himself. So unfair! There was a lot of stuff that Mr. Kim hadn't explained to me yet. Each time I would start bugging him about the *Book of Seraphim*, he would change the subject. Or tell me that I "wasn't ready yet."

I couldn't stop thinking about that night on the ship. There had been a moment when we were trapped in the cargo hold, when I thought I saw . . . Well, I'm not sure what I saw. Some-one or some*thing* standing in the smoke that was too horrible to imagine. Even now it gives me chills just thinking about it. At the time, since I was under a lot of stress, what with a real-life Dr. Evil trying to kill us and all, I figured it was my overactive imagination.

But later, when I told Mr. Kim about what I'd seen, he kind of freaked. And that alone was upsetting, because Mr. Kim doesn't freak about anything. It wasn't like he was scared. I don't think anything scares Mr. Kim, not even Simon Blankenship, who frankly scares the daylights out of me.

It was more like he got obsessed with what I thought I saw on the ship. He spent a lot of time asking me exactly what I'd seen, asking me to describe it and draw a picture of it. And he spent a lot of time running around the situation room looking at old dusty books and pulling up stuff on his computer and making all kinds of *tsk, tsk* sounds while he thought.

On the way back to my room, I kept running all this stuff over in my mind. Alex was trying to convince Brent that I had "just gotten lucky" in managing to knock down Mr. Kim, but as usual Brent wasn't talking too much. I tuned them out and thought instead about Simon trying to translate the book. My mind flashed to that thing that I saw in the smoke. It made me afraid that maybe Simon was getting some extra, otherworldly help. And that was scary in a lot of ways. At least he didn't have the real book. But I had this nagging feeling we didn't have much time before Simon made some kind of desperate move.

We reached the section of the school that splits off into the boys' and girls' wings. I waved good-bye to Alex and Brent and started toward my room.

"Hey, Raych?" It was Brent. I turned back to look at him. Alex had kept walking and was out of sight around the corner.

"Yeah?"

"I just wanted to tell you—you did really well this morning. You've improved a lot. You know how Alex likes to give you a hard time? It's all an act. He was impressed, and so was Mr. Kim. Just wanted you to know," he said. He stood there in the hallway looking all cute and Colin Farrell-y and tugging at his red *do bak* belt. For some reason I felt like blushing.

"Uh . . . thanks, Brent. Thank you," I said. As I've said, Brent was the shy, quiet type. But he had a way of saying the right things sometimes.

He nodded. "See you in Mic Elec," he said. He gave me a little mock salute, turned the corner, and was gone.

I headed to my room. One of the things I liked best about Blackthorn was my roommate, Pilar. We'd had a rocky start to our friendship. Most of it was my fault. I had a bit of an attitude when I got here. (Okay, sometimes I still do, ahem.) But we'd started to get along, with just a few little blips here and there.

One of those "blips" was her budding romance with Alex

Scott. Pilar and Alex started dating before I got to Blackthorn. Although "dating" is not exactly the right word. Nobody ever actually goes anywhere at this school. Knowing Alex and Pilar, I bet most of their "dates" consisted of meeting at the gym so they could work out and get even more exercise. Or sitting in the school library and giving each other harder math problems.

Well, since Alex and I were like oil and water, this made things a little strained between Pilar and me sometimes. I thought Alex was a big jerk and he thought I was a troublemaker. I still wasn't sure what Pilar saw in him. I mean, yeah, Alex is cute. He's tall with short blond hair and cool, almost icy blue eyes. And he's buff. I've got to give her that.

And he does have this way of looking at you where he gets this kind of dreamy expression on his face. I mean, when he really turns it on, his eyes sparkle and he gets this sort of a half-smirk on his face that makes it seem like he knows what you're thinking. And he can be funny when he's not being a jerk. He's got a really deep voice and a nice laugh.

But aside from the eyes, the laugh, the buff-ness, and his overall cuteness, I really couldn't stand being around him. Not that I thought about it a lot or anything. Well, not very often. Just once in a while. Maybe.

Hey, Spy Goddess fans!

Ever wonder how a manga gets made? Here's a little insight on what goes into bringing you the exciting Spy Goddess adventures in manga form!

The first step is developing the script. Good comics writers are visual thinkers as well as people who can set up good jokes and create touching, heartfelt moments, so their instructions to the artists should be clear, and describe dramatic scenes that are fun to illustrate. Of course, good artists will take those directions and run with them, innovating, and sometimes adding or combining panels, making sure that the visual flow works on the page. It's a team effort all around, really.

THIS IS HOW THE FIRST FEW PAGES OF SPY GODDESS 2 LOOK IN SCRIPT FORM:

PAGE 1, PANEL 1
Close on Rachel's eyes—narrow, determined.

Rachel's narration: Okay, Rachel, you barely escaped going to juvie by becoming a spy at Blackthorn Academy.

PAGE 1, PANEL 2
Close on a male figure (Mithras) partially hidden in shadows, dressed in a long, flowing black robe. Atop his head he wears a shiny silver helmet with horns protruding from it. He kneels before a large stone altar with a large, thick book resting on it. The figure appears to be offering up some kind of prayer.

Rachel's narration: And Simon Blankenship, a nut job who thinks he's the reincarnation of the bull god Mithras, has it in for you because he thinks you're the reincarnated goddess Etherea.

PAGE 1, PANEL 3
Long shot to reveal we are in a Mithrian temple—built underground and lit by torches casting a flickering glow of light across the room. Mithras is at the far end of the room, his back to us.

Rachel's narration: And now you have to kick his butt in an ancient Mithrian temple...

PAGE 1, PANEL 4
Same shot but Rachel has stepped into view (we can only see her foot and ankle)—her high-heeled, strappy shoe in the foreground, Mithras in the background.

Rachel's narration: ...with some killer Manolo Blahniks.

PAGE 2, PANEL 1
Dressed in a cute skirt and tank top and crouching behind a pew, Rachel slips on a pair of heavy-duty headphones. In this scene should she also have a really neat Coach bag or something, that she's pulling everything out of?

PAGE 2, PANEL 2
(Rachel presses a button on the sonic stun transmitter or SST—a small metallic sphere about the size of a large bouncy ball.)

FX: Click

PAGE 2, PANEL 3
Rachel rolls the ball down the aisle.

INSET
Through the eye holes in the helmet, Mithras's eyes go wide, looking off to the side where the SST just landed.

PAGE 2, PANEL 4
The ball emits a high-pitched blast.

Once the script is in order, the artist does what are called "thumbnails" or "roughs." These are meant to get the story out on the page quickly and efficiently so that the artist and editors can go over it and make sure that everything looks good and makes sense. It's harder than it seems to set up exciting scenes and make transitions from panel to panel work (it's kind of like a movie—seems simple, but there's a real art to it), so sometimes roughs go through several revisions before everyone's happy with them. Fortunately for Spy Goddess, our lovely artist really knows her stuff, and usually knocks it out of the park on the first swing.

Here are the same set of pages, now in rough form:

After the roughs are revised and approved, we go to finishes, which include inking over the pencil lines, and then filling in shadows and textures with grays and dot patterns called tones. Inking adds depth to the images, by showing volume and a bit of shadow, and tones go far beyond just "coloring" an image—they help to highlight certain moments, create the emotional effects that manga is known for, and fill in patterns and textures on the pages. See? A manga in its completed form!

DON'T MISS ALL THE BOOKS IN THE ACTION-PACKED TEEN SERIES SPY GODDESS!

SPY GODDESS, BOOK ONE: LIVE AND LET SHOP

Beverly Hills princess Rachel Buchanan has been in trouble one too many times. So she's shipped off to freaky Blackthorn Academy, a mysterious school for delinquents where the classes include Intro to Code Theory and Microelectronics. Then an ancient artifact is stolen, her headmaster disappears...and Rachel decides to find out once and for all exactly what Blackthorn Academy is hiding.

SPY GODDESS, BOOK TWO: TO HAWAII, WITH LOVE

So fourteen-year-old Rachel Buchanan is a reincarnated goddess. But, apparently, being a goddess doesn't come with any neat-o superpowers. Nope. The only thing Rachel gets is one stark-raving mad nemesis—Simon Blankenship. And the only thing standing between him and total world domination? Oh, right: Rachel. But Rachel is in luck because the next Talisman on her list is in Hawaii. Think she'll be able to fit some surfing in around saving the world?

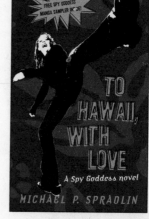